SOCCER CHAMPIONS
BY JIM WHITING

BOCA JUNIORS

CREATIVE EDUCATION • CREATIVE PAPERBACKS

Published by Creative Education
and Creative Paperbacks
P.O. Box 227, Mankato, Minnesota 56002
Creative Education and Creative Paperbacks
are imprints of The Creative Company
www.thecreativecompany.us

Design by The Design Lab; production by Darrion Hunt
Art direction by Rita Marshall
Printed in China

Photographs by Alamy (Allstar Picture Library, Canon2260, carlos cardetas, De Luan, PA Images), Creative Commons Wikimedia (Argentine Football Association Library, daledalebo, Alberto De Gasperi, Dennis1989, Estudio Van Ravenstein, El Gráfico, Revista Boca, Unknown), Getty Images (Chris Brunskill Ltd/Getty Images Sport, DANIEL LUNA/Stringer/AFP, Franco Origlia/Getty Images News, Gabriel Rossi/LatinContent WO, Bob Thomas/Bob Thomas Sports Photography), Newscom (*/Kyodo, CHINE NOUVELLE/SIPA, Jaime Echeverria/EFE, Juan Ignacio Roncoroni/EFE, TELAM/Xinhua News Agency, [e] MARTIN ZABALA/Xinhua News Agency), Shutterstock (gualtiero boffi, Filipe Frazao, R-O-M-A)

Copyright © 2019 Creative Education, Creative Paperbacks
International copyright reserved in all countries. No part of this book may be reproduced in any form without written permission from the publisher.

Library of Congress Cataloging-in-Publication Data
Names: Whiting, Jim, author.
Title: Boca Juniors / Jim Whiting.
Series: Soccer champions.
Includes bibliographical references and index.
Summary: A chronicle of the people, matches, and world events that shaped the South American men's Argentine soccer team known as Boca Juniors, from its founding in 1905 to today.
Identifiers: LCCN 2017059836
ISBN 978-1-60818-977-9 (hardcover)
ISBN 978-1-62832-604-8 (pbk)
ISBN 978-1-64000-078-0 (eBook)
LCSH: 1. Boca Juniors (Soccer club)—History—Juvenile literature. 2. Soccer players—Argentina—Biography—Juvenile literature.

Classification: LCC GV943.6.B59 W55 20185 / DDC 796.3340982—dc23

CCSS: RI.5.1, 2, 3, 8; RH.6-8.4, 5, 7

First Edition HC 9 8 7 6 5 4 3 2 1
First Edition PBK 9 8 7 6 5 4 3 2 1

Cover and page 3: Midfielder Fernando Gago
Page 1: 2015 Copa Libertadores

6
INTRODUCTION

10
THE BIRTH OF BOCA

14
GAINING RECOGNITION

20
PLAY FOR PAY

24
THE MARADONA "ERA"

30
DOWN AND BACK UP ... WAY UP

36
MEMORABLE MATCHES TIMELINE
December 23, 1928 v. River Plate
September 20, 1931 v. River Plate
March 17, 1971 v. Sporting Cristal
March 21 and August 1, 1978
v. Borussia Mönchengladbach
November 28, 2000 v. Real Madrid
June 10 and 17, 2004 v. River Plate

40
FAMOUS FOOTBALLERS
Serverino Varela
Antonio Rattín
Silvio Marzolini
Martín Palermo
Juan Román Riquelme
Carlos Tevez

Boca Juniors Titles 44
Selected Bibliography 46
Websites 47
Index 48

CONTENTS

Forward Carlos Tevez

INTRODUCTION

Soccer (or football, as it is known almost everywhere outside of the United States) is truly a universal game. Originating in Europe, it quickly spread to the rest of the world. The Fédération Internationale de Football Association (FIFA), the international governing body of soccer, is divided into six confederations. The Confederación Sudamericana de Fútbol (CONMEBOL) regulates soccer in South America. Nearly every country has at least one league with several divisions. At the end of each season, the bottommost teams in one division are relegated (moved down) to the next lower division, while the same number of topmost teams from that lower division move up to replace them. This ensures a consistently high level of competition. Late-season games between teams with losing records still feature spirited competition as both sides seek to avoid relegation.

Founded as the Argentine Association Football League (AAFL) in 1893, the renamed Asociación del Fútbol Argentino (AFA) organizes leagues in Argentina. The season concludes with a champion determined by points gained throughout the season. Teams receive three points for a win and one point for a tie. The top league in Argentina is the Superliga Argentina. Long known as the Primera División, it has undergone a number of format changes during its

Boca Juniors has been one of the most successful teams in the history of the Primera División.

history. Some of these changes resulted in two separate competitions being held the same year. This created the opportunity for clubs to win two league championships in one year. Currently, the Superliga holds its annual tournament from August to June. It has historically been dominated by the "Big Five," all of which are based in the Greater Buenos Aires area: River Plate, Boca Juniors, Independiente, Racing Club, and San Lorenzo de Almagro. In recent years, however, other teams have risen to challenge the Big Five.

Another significant championship is the national cup, or Copa Argentina. Originally contested in 1969 and 1970, it was re-established in 2011. Copa Argentina is similar to England's FA Cup or Spain's Copa del Rey. It includes more than 200 teams. The schedule is spread out over nine months, and games are played at neutral sites. The champion takes on the Superliga winner in the Supercopa Argentina.

Continent-wide competitions include Copa Sudamericana, which began in 2002 and now fields up to 50 teams. The Recopa Sudamericana pits the Copa Sudamericana champion against the winner of CONMEBOL's prestigious Copa Libertadores de América. Dating back to 1960, Libertadores is generally regarded as being on a competitive par with Europe's Champions League. It begins with nearly 50 teams and consists of 6 rounds of competition. The winner also plays in the FIFA Club World Cup, an annual seven-team tournament. It includes the top team from each of the six confederations and the host nation. The winner is universally regarded as world champion.

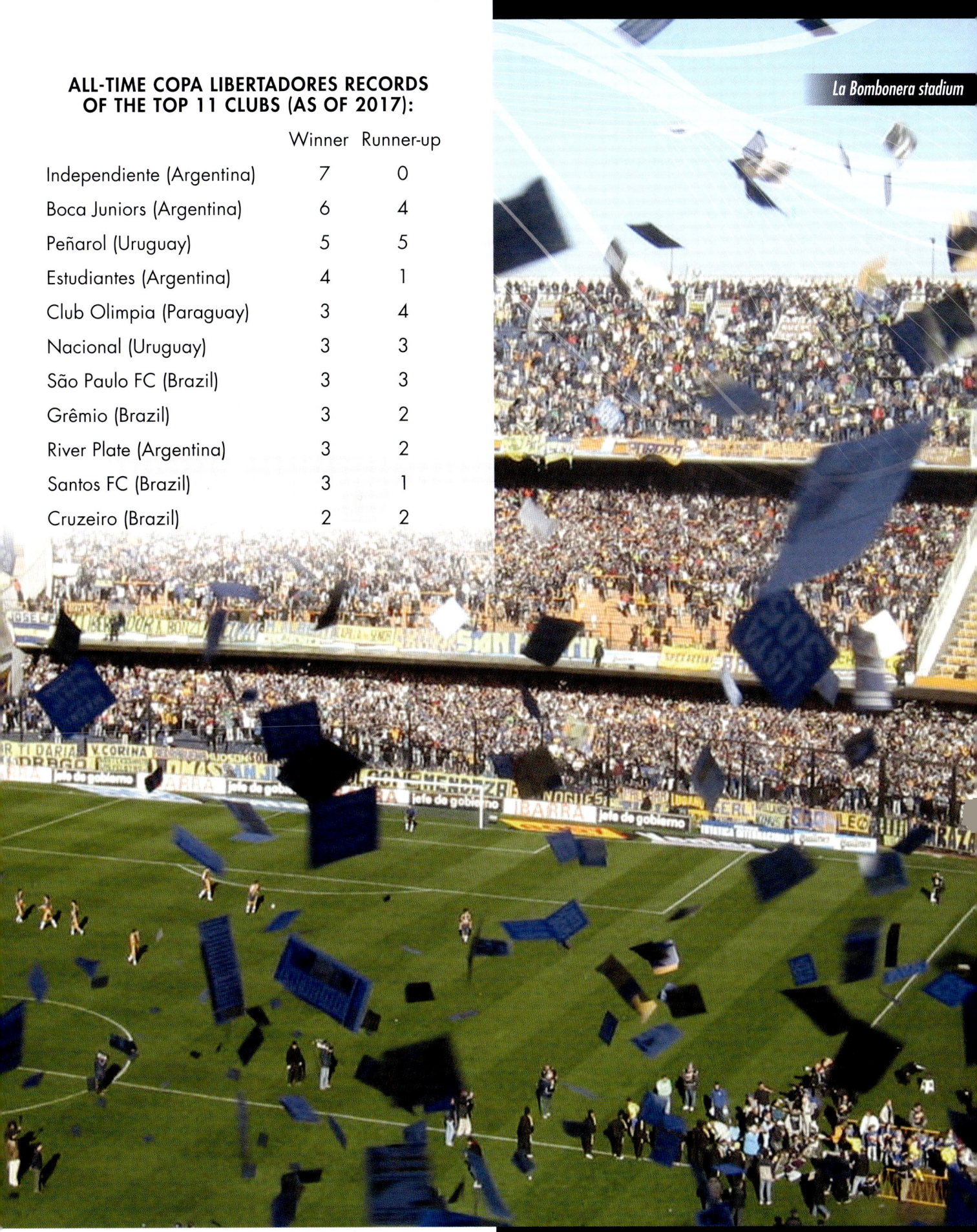

ALL-TIME COPA LIBERTADORES RECORDS OF THE TOP 11 CLUBS (AS OF 2017):

	Winner	Runner-up
Independiente (Argentina)	7	0
Boca Juniors (Argentina)	6	4
Peñarol (Uruguay)	5	5
Estudiantes (Argentina)	4	1
Club Olimpia (Paraguay)	3	4
Nacional (Uruguay)	3	3
São Paulo FC (Brazil)	3	3
Grêmio (Brazil)	3	2
River Plate (Argentina)	3	2
Santos FC (Brazil)	3	1
Cruzeiro (Brazil)	2	2

La Bombonera stadium

THE BIRTH OF BOCA

Increasing trade during the 19th century helped Buenos Aires to flourish.

In the late 19th and early 20th centuries, thousands of Italians made the long ocean crossing to settle in Argentina. Many of the newcomers settled in La Boca, a neighborhood in Buenos Aires. *Boca* means "mouth" in Spanish. It refers to the neighborhood's location at the outlet of the Matanza River, where dockyards provided plenty of employment opportunities for the immigrants. When they weren't working, the men enjoyed sports. One of their favorite games was soccer.

Another newcomer, Irishman Paddy McCarthy, arrived in 1900. He began teaching English and sports at a school in the area. He achieved local fame in 1903 for promoting and participating in Argentina's first professional boxing match, even though it was illegal. The local police chief served as timekeeper, which no doubt helped safeguard the fight. McCarthy won the match.

At that time, sports were largely associated with well-to-do Argentinians. McCarthy is credited with encouraging working-class youngsters to take up soccer. On April 3, 1905, three of his soccer-playing students—Esteban Baglietto, Santiago Sana, and Alfredo Scarpatti—met with brothers Teodoro and Juan Antonio Farenga at Baglietto's house to form a soccer team. After listening to the boisterous teens for several hours, Baglietto's father kicked them out. They continued their discussion in La Plaza Solís. The square was La Boca's first public plaza and a popular gathering place. Today, it is commonly regarded as the birthplace of Boca Juniors. A plaque commemorates the occasion.

The teens took their neighborhood as the team name. Because of the popularity of English names in Argentina, they chose "Juniors" as the nickname. The boys rounded up enough friends to form a full team and played their first game just 18 days after their meeting. They set the tone for Boca's future with a 4–0 win. The Farenga brothers tallied three of the points; Sana added the fourth.

For the team's first games, the Farengas' sister, Manuela, sewed vertical black stripes onto white shirts. But they hit a snag two years later. Another team had virtually the same design. Different teams couldn't have the same kit. So, to resolve the issue, they agreed to play a game. The winner would keep the black-and-white stripes, and the loser would switch. Boca lost. Team member Juan Brichetto suggested that they adopt the colors of the flag of the first ship to enter the

In their first team photo in 1906, the players wore white shirts with vertical stripes.

harbor the following morning. The next day, the young men watched as a vessel drew steadily nearer, until they spotted its blue and yellow Swedish flag swirling in the breeze.

Because so many people in Boca had come from the Italian city of Genoa, the team quickly added its enduring nickname: "los Xeneizes" (the Genoese). The team's new colors generated another nickname: "Azul y Oro" (Blue and Gold). A third nickname, "La Mitad Más Uno" (The Half Plus One), came years later when the team rose to its peak of popularity. It refers to the team's claim to be supported by more than half of Argentina.

A less-flattering nickname soon arose. Boca's stadium was on the site of a former brick factory. Brickmaking required large quantities of manure, which permeated the neighborhood with its foul odor. The Spanish word for manure is *bosta*. Since

the word sounds somewhat similar to *boca*, opposing fans loved to chant "*Bosteros! Bosteros! Bosteros!*" (manure handlers) during games. Over the years, however, Bosteros lost its negative connotation. Today, Boca fans embrace the nickname.

Boca began what would become one of the greatest legacies in South American soccer by playing in lower-level leagues. It won championships in both the Villa Lobos League and the Liga Albión. The team took a giant step forward when it joined the AFA in 1908. It played in Segunda de Ascenso, the second-level division. Winning its first game against Club Atlético Belgrano was a sign of things to come. The next goal for the Xeneizes was promotion to the Primera División, the country's top league. When the division expanded in 1913, Boca was one of the teams to be added. On August 24 of that year, Boca played a match that would initiate perhaps the most heated rivalry in all of soccer.

GAINING RECOGNITION

Since joining the Primera División in 1913, Boca has never been relegated.

In 1901, two other soccer teams in La Boca had merged to form a club called River Plate. When River and Boca played for the first time in 1913 (reports of matches as early as 1908 are unsubstantiated), fights broke out. A Boca player was sidelined early in the second half by an injury resulting from the violence. About 25 minutes later, the referee tossed a River player out of the game. River won, 2–1.

Marcos Mayer had the distinction of scoring the first Boca goal in what would

The team's old stadium was demolished in the late 1930s to make way for La Bombonera.

become known as the Superclásico. *Clásico* means "classic" in Spanish, and "super" reflects the teams' status as the most popular in Argentina. The *Daily Telegraph* labels the Superclásico as "the biggest club rivalry in world football." The soccer magazine *FourFourTwo* agrees, calling it "the biggest derby in the world." (A "derby" in soccer is a rivalry between two teams from the same city or region.) In 2004, the *Observer* put the Superclásico first on its list of "50 Sporting Things You Must Do Before You Die."

"River and Boca dominate the Argentine football landscape," notes Joel Richards, author of *Superclásico: Inside the Ultimate Derby*. "The fixture … is in many ways a mirror of the game in Argentina, mined of its raw talent, relying on the hard sell, yet rich with tradition, thick with intrigue, strong on drama, and with the occasional flash of brilliance on the pitch."

"In Superclásico week, [Buenos Aires] stops being just another pretty South American capital city, and becomes a football town: a stage for a sporting showdown in which no one remains neutral," the *Independent* adds. It's not just the Argentine capital that becomes involved. TVs throughout the country are tuned to the game. The appeal extends beyond the country's borders, too. According to a 2012 report, more than 120 million people around the world watched the Superclásico. The only derby with a larger audience is El Clásico, which pits FC Barcelona against its fellow Spanish giant, Real Madrid.

Violence is common, both on and off the field. Typically, more than 1,000 police officers are summoned to protect spectators. They are not always successful. Two River fans were shot and killed after a 2–0 victory in 1994. With a TV camera in his face, a Boca supporter gleefully declared, "We tied 2–2." The rivalry even extends beyond death. As he lay dying, a lifelong Boca fan asked to be wrapped in a River flag. That way, he explained, he could take "one of them" with him.

Despite losing to River, Boca placed a respectable fifth in its first Primera División season. The Xeneizes improved to 3rd in 1914, only to tumble to 14th in the following 2 seasons. Their 7–0 loss to San Isidro in 1915 remains the worst drubbing in team history. They rebounded to place fourth in 1917 and third in 1918. The latter season also marked Boca's first victory over River.

Midway through the following season, 14 teams split off to form the Asociación Amateurs de Football (AAmF). River jumped to the AAmF,

Opposite: Mario Boyé was a scoring threat for Boca in the 1940s; murals in Buenos Aires (pictured) reflect the popularity of the team today.

but Boca stayed put. As a result, the rivals didn't meet for several years. Boca won the league title in 1919 and defended it the following season. After two third-place finishes, Boca returned to the top in 1923 and 1924.

The 1924 win was especially noteworthy. As the league expanded to 22 teams, Boca had one of the most dominant seasons in Primera División history. The Xeneizes won 18 of 19 games and tied the other. In just over a decade, the new kids on the block had become the biggest kids on the block.

Buoyed by its remarkable success, the team embarked on a European tour in 1925—something virtually unheard of in that era. The traveling party included a super-fan, Victoriano "Toto" Caffarena, who not only paid his own way but also helped out by giving massages and taking care of the uniforms. The players appreciated his efforts so much that they called him *el jugador número 12* (the player number 12). Today, Boca fans refer to themselves as "La 12," effectively identical to the "12th Man" concept claimed by football fans of Texas A&M University and the Seattle Seahawks.

The European tour was successful; Boca won 15 games, lost 3, and tied 1. The AFA designated the players "Champions of Honor" for their success. Because the

Boca Juniors was among 18 teams to go from amateur to professional status in 1931.

tour occurred during much of the league season, Boca played just seven league games. Winning six and tying one, it still finished ahead of three teams that played a full slate of games. In 1926, Boca picked up where it had left off. It went 15–0–2 in the AFA, scoring 67 goals and conceding only 4 for yet another title.

The AFA and the AAmF merged in 1927. Boca finished second in the 34-team league. The merger also marked the resumption of the heated rivalry with River. Boca claimed a 1–0 victory that year. Then the Xeneizes completely dismantled River in 1928. Their 6–0 win still marks the largest victory margin for either team. Boca broke through to win the league in 1930. An even greater transformation of Argentine soccer was about to begin.

PLAY FOR PAY

By this time, soccer was increasing in popularity throughout much of South America. Increased popularity meant increased club income in the form of ticket sales. While soccer was still officially an amateur sport, that didn't stop clubs from compensating players under the table. They were paid in the form of cash and merchandise such as expensive clothing. This gave players a certain amount of flexibility. They could flit from one club to another, seeking the best deals. In addition, professional European clubs began luring away the best players with lucrative contracts.

So, in 1931, there was another split in Argentine soccer. Eighteen clubs formed the openly professional Liga Argentina de Football (LAF). The rest remained with the AFA. Both leagues were considered part of the Primera División, but they held separate championships. The players' game of musical chairs ended as they signed contracts binding them to a team. Boca took the first LAF title with a controversial win over River.

By then the rivalry had taken on yet another dimension. While Boca proudly stayed in the area of its founding, River had moved to a more upscale neighborhood. As a result, people began to regard Boca as the "people's team," whereas River was increasingly associated with the well-to-do of Buenos Aires. River took top honors in the Primera División in 1932. That set the stage for the next 15 years, with River winning 7 more titles and Boca 5. Boca

Estadio Alberto J. Armando, commonly known as La Bombonera, seats 49,000 people.

was second by a single point in 1933. It then became the first team to score 100 goals in a season as it won the league in 1934. At the end of that season, the AFA and LAF merged.

The 1940 championship season was especially memorable for Boca. To recognize the importance of professional soccer in the country's daily life, the Argentine government had extended loans to teams. River had already taken advantage of this program to open El Monumental, the country's largest soccer facility, in 1938. At the same time, Boca began building what would become the team's iconic home pitch, La Bombonera. The name means "the chocolate box." Reportedly, the designer pointed out the similarity of the shape of a box of chocolates to the stadium's contours. It is a tiered horseshoe shape, with the fourth side forming a thin, flat, almost vertical grandstand consisting largely of VIP boxes. Boca won the first game in its new facility in May 1940. Ricardo Alarcón scored the first goals at La Bombonera.

In 1942, Boca registered its largest-ever win. The Xeneizes scored twice in the opening 10 minutes against relegation-bound Club Atlético Tigre. They added four more tallies in the first half. They hit the back of the net twice more midway through the second half and finished with 3 goals in the final 10 minutes. Julio Jorge Rosell and Rubén Marcial Barrios both scored hat tricks in the 11–1 rout. Boca scored only 54 goals

Ricardo Alarcón (opposite) was one of many Boca stars to play in Superclásico (above), the heated rivalry between Boca Juniors and River Plate.

in the rest of the season. It finished fifth. The team rebounded to win the league in 1943 and 1944. The latter season included a streak of 26 games without a loss, an AFA record that would last for more than 20 years.

That year also marked the team's last title for a decade. In 1949, Boca was nearly relegated. The Xeneizes secured a 5–1 win in the season's final game to stay in the Primera División. They placed second the following year and finally claimed the cup again in 1954. A key player was goalie Julio Elías Musimessi. He was known as *el arquero cantor* (the singing goalkeeper) for his radio performances. One of the multitalented keeper's grandsons, Lionel Messi, would become one of the world's greatest soccer players of all time.

THE MARADONA "ERA"

Boca did not win another Primera División title until 1962. The key to that season's success was defense. Two standouts were defender Silvio Marzolini and goalkeeper Antonio Roma. Roma was nicknamed "Tarzan" because of the way he flung himself at the ball. Boca earned the championship with a 1–0 victory over River at La Bombonera in the season's next-to-last game. Roma swatted away a late penalty kick to seal the win. Jubilant fans rushed onto the field. It took nearly 15 minutes to shepherd them back into the stands. The Xeneizes did even better 2 years later, giving up just 15 goals in 30 games. In between those seasons, in 1963, they

Goalkeeper Antonio Roma's most famous save came during a crucial game against River in 1962.

advanced to the finals of the Copa Libertadores for the first time, falling to Brazil's Santos FC, 5–3 on aggregate.

In 1968, Boca suffered the worst disaster in Argentine football. After a game at River's El Monumental, 71 people were killed as they piled up against one another at a closed gate known as Puerta (Door) 12. Another 150 were injured. A lengthy investigation failed to determine the cause of the Puerta 12 tragedy. Various theories blamed River fans, the police, and even the Boca fans themselves. Since the tragedy,

Defender Julio Meléndez helped Boca capture Primera División titles in 1969 and 1970.

Boca was a powerhouse in 1977, taking both the Copa Libertadores (opposite) and the Intercontinental Cup.

Parados: Mouzo, Veglio, Ovide, Alves, Pernia, Biasuto, Diaz, Gatti, Quintieri (masajista). Sentados: Lacava Schell, Gutiérre Ribolzi, Taverna, Tarantini.

BOCA

Suñé, Mastrángelo, Favret,

gates at El Monumental have been identified by letters rather than numbers, but nothing else changed.

The following year, Roma kept a clean sheet for an astounding 783 minutes—nearly 9 games—as Boca yielded only 11 goals en route to another Primera División championship. It repeated the title in 1970.

The Xeneizes began an especially productive, albeit short-term, soccer success story in 1976. In a Primera División format change, Boca won both the Metropolitano and Nacional championships. Boca was fourth in its group during the initial round of the Metropolitano but went undefeated in the final round. It won the Nacional in the best possible way, defeating River in the championship game. Rubén Suñé scored the game's only point on a free kick midway through the second half.

That victory qualified the Xeneizes for the 1977 Copa Libertadores, where they faced Cruzeiro of Brazil. The teams traded 1–0 wins. A third game at a neutral site ended 0–0 and went to penalty kicks. It nearly began disastrously for Boca. Roberto Mouzo hit the right upright as the Cruzeiro goalkeeper lunged in the opposite direction. But the referee ruled that the keeper had left his line prematurely. Given a second chance, Mouzo didn't miss. Then, with Boca ahead by one, goalkeeper Hugo Gatti got both hands on Cruzeiro's final shot and easily deflected it.

That victory led to Boca's second major international trophy. It defeated Germany's Borussia Mönchengladbach in the 1977 Intercontinental Cup to become the unofficial world champion. (The Intercontinental Cup was the forerunner of the Club World Cup.) Hoping to defend its Copa Libertadores title, Boca faced Deportivo Cali of Colombia. After a scoreless tie in Colombia, the Xeneizes overwhelmed Deportivo Cali 4–0 at La Bombonera. Boca sought a three-peat in 1979, but lost on aggregate to Club Olimpia of Paraguay.

Two years later, Boca signed attacking midfielder Diego Maradona. Even though he was barely 20, he was the most famous active player in South America—if not in the entire world. Maradona was a prodigy who was discovered when he was only eight years old. "We asked for his ID card so we could check it," said Francis Cornejo, his youth coach. "Although he had the physique of a child, he played like an adult." Maradona began playing professionally for Argentinos Juniors when he was 15. He led the league in scoring five times. He was still a teenager in 1979 when the Spanish powerhouse FC Barcelona made him an offer. The AFA gave Argentinos nearly half a million dollars to pay Maradona enough to stay home.

When Maradona joined Boca, he scored 28 goals in 40 games. "I wanted Diego to settle in quickly and feel comfortable, so that we could enjoy him and get the best from him," said Mouzo. "It had become 'Diego's Boca.'… I tried to give him more confidence, so we could use him more effectively, so I gave him the captaincy." The Xeneizes won their first Primera División title in five years. But Maradona left for Barcelona after that single season for a world-record transfer fee.

Diego Maradona was hailed as a hero when Boca topped the Primera División in 1981.

DOWN AND BACK UP ... WAY UP

Maradona's departure was the start of nearly two lean decades. The team struggled with financial issues, and its only Primera División victory came in 1992. Maradona returned to Boca in 1995 in the twilight of what some people consider to be one of the greatest careers in soccer history. But he struggled with drug issues and was out

Maradona returned to Boca Juniors in 1995 but struggled with personal problems.

30

After a slump in the mid-1990s, Boca was rejuvenated by the end of the decade.

of shape. He had little effect on the team's performance. Maradona played his final game in 1997. He asked to be removed at halftime. His replacement was 19-year-old Juan Román Riquelme, who sparked the Xeneizes to a 2–1 victory over River. It was a symbolic moment. If Maradona had stayed with Boca, he would have been the greatest player in team history. Many people now believe that Riquelme deserves that status.

The following season, Carlos Bianchi became coach. He instilled 10 commandments for his players, which included 8 hours of sleep at night, a 2-hour siesta, and a ban on cell phones during practice. It paid off immediately. Boca won the league's Apertura tournament that year and its Clausura tournament early in 1999. During that

Boca Juniors overcame Real Madrid, 2–1, in 2000 to win its second Club World Cup.

span, the club was unbeaten in a staggering 40 games, a Primera División record that remained unbroken as of 2018.

The team also began to regularly take on the powerhouses of European soccer in the Intercontinental Cup (renamed the Toyota Cup). Despite being heavy underdogs, Boca knocked off Spain's Real Madrid in 2000. It nearly defeated Germany's Bayern Munich the following year. A spectacular save in the first half by Bayern goalkeeper Oliver Kahn preserved a scoreless tie. The game went to overtime, and the Germans emerged with the win after netting a goal in the 109th minute.

Two years later, Boca faced Italy's AC Milan. The teams traded goals in the first half. The game came down to penalty kicks. Milan converted just one of four, and Boca won. The Italians were bitter. "We played a great game and were better than the Argentinians, but we didn't convert our chances," said one Milan player. They certainly were better in 2007. The two teams met again in

33

what was now known as the FIFA Club World Cup. Milan scored three times in the second half for a 4–2 victory. Earlier that year, Boca won the Copa Libertadores for the sixth time, placing it second overall to Independiente.

Since then, Boca has added four more Primera División crowns to its already bulging trophy case. The most recent came in 2017. After defeating Santa Fe in the final game of the season amidst a raucous display of fireworks, streamers, and screams from legions of passionate fans, Boca officials unveiled an addition to La Bombonera. It is an enormous clock that displays the years, days, hours, and minutes since the Xeneizes had been relegated. That is to say—never. It is a continuing display of dominance and excellence. The team's total of 32 Primera División titles ranks second only to River's 36 (as of 2018).

Boca Juniors is one of the world's most successful football clubs. It has won 22 international tournaments, 18 of which are recognized by FIFA. That ties the Xeneizes for fourth with AC Milan among the hundreds of clubs throughout the globe. Fans at La Bombonera look forward to the relegation clock continuing to count up the minutes, hours, days, and years long into the future.

In 2017, midfielder Wilmar Barrios (16) helped Boca win its 32nd Primera División title.

MEMORABLE MATCHES

1900   **1910**   **1920**   **1930**

1905
Team was founded.

1928
Boca Juniors v. River Plate
Superclásico, December 23, 1928, Buenos Aires, Argentina

In the teams' second meeting since the merger of the AFA and the AAmF, Boca got off to a fast start. Domingo Tarasconi scored just three minutes into the game. A little later, two River players collided, banging their heads together. Both had to leave the field. River had no substitutes, so it had to play down two men. Boca's Esteban Kuko scored 10 minutes later, and Tarasconi added another goal just before halftime. Kuko rammed home a goal early in the second half. Then Roberto Cherro made it 5–0. Yet another River player limped off soon afterward. Cherro took advantage to score his second goal. With less than 10 minutes remaining, the River captain asked the referee to end the match to avoid further humiliation. "Boca is a claw. Insurance in all its positions, strong in defense, and very dangerous in attack; you are sweeping their opponents in final form," reported the newspaper *Última Hora* the following day. Nearly a century later, Boca's 6–0 victory remains the most one-sided result in Superclásico history.

1940   1950   1960   1970

1931
Boca Juniors v. River Plate
Superclásico, September 20, 1931, Buenos Aires, Argentina

The first meeting between Boca and River in the professional era was a case of the same old bitter rivalry. River scored first. Thirteen minutes later, Boca winger Francisco Varallo was taken down inside the penalty box. River goalie Jorge Iribarren partially blocked Varallo's penalty kick. As the two men scrambled for the loose ball, Varallo decked his opponent, then nudged the ball into the open net to tie the score. River players went ballistic and swarmed the hapless referee, Enrique Escola. He sent off three of them. But they refused to leave. Moments later, Escola called off the match. Irate fans flooded onto the field. They met a wall of mounted police, who swung clubs and doused them with tear gas. Three weeks later, league officials awarded Boca the victory. By the time he left the team in 1940, Varallo was Boca's all-time leading scorer in Primera División play, with 181 goals. His mark stood for nearly 70 years.

1971
Boca Juniors v. Sporting Cristal
Copa Libertadores First Round, March 17, 1971, Buenos Aires, Argentina

Both teams were in the hunt to advance to the second round. In the split home game setup, Cristal had taken the first match on its home pitch in Peru. Late in this game, the score was tied, 2–2. Sporting Cristal felt that Boca midfielder Roberto Rogel had flopped to the ground in an attempt to draw a foul. That would set up a potential game-winning free kick. The players began shoving each other. The fighting quickly escalated despite police efforts to restore order. Players threw punches that drew blood and caused several of them to be taken to the hospital. One even grabbed the stick holding a corner flag and tried to spear an opponent. All but three players—two of whom were keepers—were sent off. The remainder of the match was canceled, and Boca was disqualified from the rest of the tournament. The brawl's aftermath was surprisingly peaceful. Most of the players had been taken to jail, where they shared pizza with each other.

37

1978

Boca Juniors v. Borussia Mönchengladbach

1977 Intercontinental Cup, March 21, 1978, Buenos Aires, Argentina, and August 1, 1978, Karlsruhe, Germany

The European Cup champion Liverpool FC declined to participate, so Boca took on the German runner-up. Scheduling issues pushed the games into the following year. In the opening game, two Borussia goals in quick succession gave Germany a 2–1 lead. Boca equalized early in the second half, and the game ended 2–2. The Germans felt confident with the next game at home. Their best player was returning from an injury that had caused him to miss the first game. But Boca forward Darío Felman stunned the host team with a goal two minutes into the game. Goalkeeper Hugo Gatti, who hadn't played in the first game, made several saves to preserve the lead. Striker Ernesto Mastrángelo scored the easiest goal of his career half an hour later when the ball wound up at his feet, just a few inches from the goal. He tapped it home. Midfielder Carlos Horacio Salinas all but iced the game four minutes later. Borussia mounted a furious rally, but Gatti maintained his clean sheet as Boca claimed the cup.

2000

2010

2000
Boca Juniors v. Real Madrid
Toyota Cup, November 28, 2000, Tokyo, Japan

Under new sponsorship from 1980 to 2004, the Intercontinental Cup moved to Japan and became a single game. Real was the overwhelming favorite, set to win its second title in three years and continue the recent European domination of the cup. But Boca refused to be intimidated by the Spanish giant's towering reputation. Martín Palermo shocked Real by scoring two minutes into the game and again three minutes later. Real dominated play for the rest of the game. But it couldn't overcome Palermo's early scores. He was named Man of the Match. Many people thought the honor belonged to Juan Román Riquelme, who skillfully orchestrated his team's play and continually frustrated Real's efforts. Diego Maradona said, "Riquelme played the sort of football which we Argentinians like and which really typifies the South American style." Riquelme deflected such post-game praise. "The whole team played magnificently," he said. "All I did was play my part." As he celebrated his team's victory, coach Carlos Bianchi added, "We knew very well who we were up against, but we also knew we were a match for anyone. We weren't cocky, and we won the title deservedly."

2004
Boca Juniors v. River Plate
Copa Libertadores Semifinal, June 10 and 17, 2004, Buenos Aires, Argentina

The Boca-River rivalry may have reached its peak in these two games. Boca won the first match, 1–0. Two River players and one Boca were expelled. The Xeneizes were fortunate not to lose more. Goalie Roberto Abbondanzieri tried to choke a River player, while striker Guillermo Barros Schelotto assaulted a River trainer. Neither was ejected. The red tide continued the following week. A Boca player was tossed midway through the second half, and a River player followed him soon afterward, along with much of the coaching staff because of the vehemence of their protests. River took the lead, but Boca's Carlos Tevez evened the score. River scored again to knot the aggregate at 2–2. Boca won on penalty kicks. The game is perhaps best remembered for Tevez's "chicken dance" after his goal. He ripped off his shirt and flapped his arms. River had long been nicknamed "gallinas" (chickens) because of their supposed tendency to choke at crucial moments in important games. Tevez was sent off. "The passion got the best of me," he said after the game. "I apologize to the River fans."

39

FAMOUS FOOTBALLERS

SEVERINO VARELA

(1913-95)
Striker, 1942-45

Severino Varela was noted for wearing a white beret during games. He was also noted for taking a ferry after Boca's Sunday games back to his home in Montevideo, Uruguay, where he worked in a factory during the week. He scored so often during his first season that Boca offered him a much larger contract—if he would move to Buenos Aires to train with the team. Varela turned it down. He didn't want to leave his friends and his job. Varela entered the pantheon of Boca heroes in September 1943 during a Superclásico. River held a 1–0 lead when the referee awarded Boca a free kick. Rather than taking a direct shot, Boca's Carlos Sosa directed a high, arching pass toward the goal. Varela launched himself into the air and headed the ball into the net. He also scored what proved to be the winning goal in the second half. But it was the first one—christened *el golazo del misterio* (the goal of mystery) by a local newspaper—that endeared him to Boca fans. Boca won the Primera División by a single point that year. Many fans credited Varela's goal with making the victory possible.

ANTONIO RATTÍN

(1937–)
Midfielder, 1956–70

Antonio Rattín is a rarity among elite soccer players. He played his entire career with a single team. In his heyday, Rattín was regarded as the game's best defensive midfielder. He set the tone for his career in his first game, against River Plate and its legendary forward Ángel Labruna. "In the fifth minute, I kicked *el Feo* [the Ugly One] incredibly hard," he recalled. When Labruna protested, Rattín mockingly replied, "I'm so sorry, Ángel. I didn't mean to do that." He is most famous for an incident in the 1966 World Cup, played in England. During a game with the host nation, Rattín—who was the Argentine captain—was dismissed. The German referee, who knew no Spanish, cited Rattín for "violence of the tongue." Furious, Rattín plopped down on a red carpet reserved for the exclusive use of the Queen. Two policemen escorted him to the dressing room. Because of the shock generated by this breach of propriety—along with his dark features—he may inadvertently have helped English mothers get their youngsters to eat their vegetables. "If you don't," they would say ominously, "Rattín will visit you in the night."

SILVIO MARZOLINI

(1940–)
Defender, 1960–72
Manager, 1981

Marzolini played a key role during Boca's success in the 1960s. As he explained, Boca was "a strong team based on a tight defense so that when we scored once, the game ended." No one was more vital to this "tight defense" than Marzolini himself. Many people regard him as the best left back in Argentine football history. He began his youth career at the age of 15 and joined Boca 5 years later. He played in 408 games, putting him third on Boca's all-time list. He also coached Boca to the 1981 Metropolitano title (one of two Primera División championships that year). Marzolini was ahead of his time. Author Jonathan Wilson calls him "the heartthrob of his day, the first Argentinian soccer player to really to exploit his commercial potential … [An advertising poster] showed Marzolini in Argentina uniform, blond hair neatly parted, blue eyes smoldering at the camera." In today's market, Marzolini would likely command the same kinds of multimillion-dollar endorsement deals as Cristiano Ronaldo and Neymar.

MARTÍN PALERMO

(1973–)
Striker, 1997–2000, 2004–11

Martín Palermo is Boca's all-time leading scorer, with 236 goals in 404 appearances. He scored both goals in Boca's 2–1 win over Real Madrid in the 2000 Intercontinental Cup and was named Man of the Match. That brought him to the attention of Spanish clubs. He spent four largely frustrating years in Spain, thanks to injuries. He returned to Boca, where he regained his health and spent the rest of his career. Many of his goals were memorable. Once he scored from just inside his own half of the field. His 100th goal helped Boca win the 2004 Copa Sudamericana. His 200th was a game-winning header from more than 40 yards out. At the age of 36, he became the oldest Argentine player to score in a World Cup. Unfortunately, Palermo is most noted for goals he *didn't* score. In a 1999 Copa América game against Colombia, he missed three penalty kicks. Argentina lost 3–0. But Palermo was resilient. He scored a goal in his next game, three days later.

JUAN ROMÁN RIQUELME

(1978–)
Attacking midfielder, 1996–2002, 2007, 2008–14

Riquelme is regarded as one of the greatest—if not *the* greatest—Boca players. He once said that his workweek began on Monday and ended on Saturday, "because on Sundays I can't really call it work, I enjoy playing the matches so much." Though he grew up in poverty, Riquelme was surrounded by *potreros*—vacant lots where countless Argentine youngsters develop their soccer skills. He made his debut with Boca when he was 18. He helped the team win two Copa Libertadores and three Primera División titles before heading to Spain. Just before leaving, his 17-year-old brother Cristián was kidnapped. Fortunately, the teen was released unharmed when Riquelme paid the ransom. Riquelme's European experience was mixed—he barely played for Barcelona, yet spurred Villarreal to the semifinals of the Champions League before returning home and playing for Boca until his retirement. He was often compared to a quarterback, determining the pace and direction of the action. Sports columnist Horacio Pagani said Riquelme was "the second inventor of football; the first were the English over one hundred years ago."

CARLOS TEVEZ

(1984–)
Forward, 2001–04, 2015–16, 2018–present

As a child, Tevez was severely scalded by boiling water, landing him in intensive care for several months and leaving him with a livid scar. After joining Boca at 16, he refused the club's offer to remove it, saying that it was part of his identity. The scar had no effect on his playing ability. He was named South American Footballer of the Year twice during his time with Boca. He was also named Copa Libertadores Most Valuable Player in 2003 as he led Boca to the championship. Tevez played in Europe for a decade before returning to Boca in 2015 to realize his long-held dream of winning the Primera División. He also helped Boca win the Copa Argentina later that year. Earlier in 2015 he had achieved the same double with his European club, Juventus of Italy. That made him the first soccer player to win two domestic leagues and two domestic cups in the same calendar year. In December 2016, he scored twice as Boca beat River in the Superclásico. Shortly afterward, he signed with the Chinese club Shanghai Shenhua for a reported $41-million salary, making him among the world's highest-paid soccer players. Following a disastrous year, Tevez again rejoined the Xeneizes in January 2018.

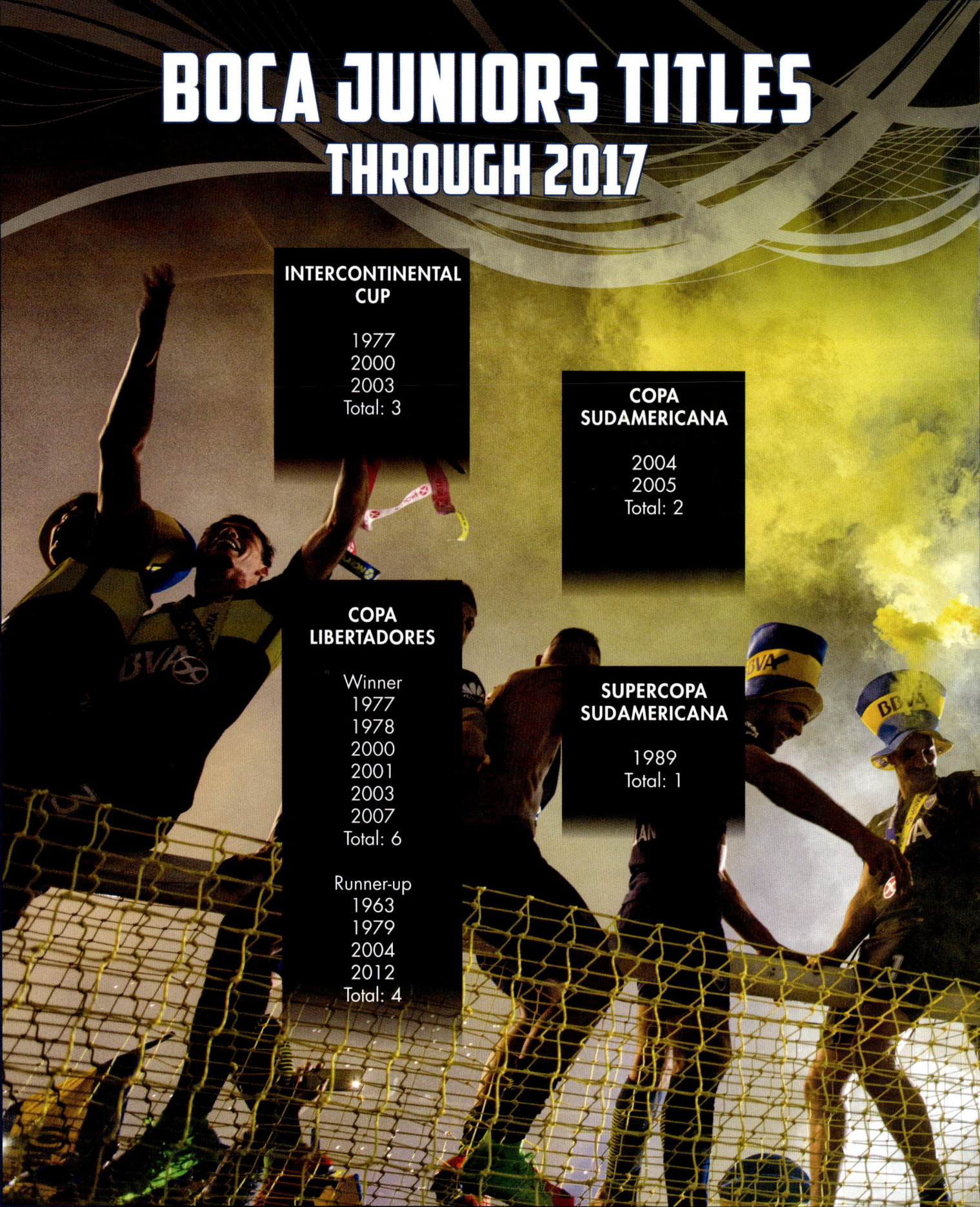

BOCA JUNIORS TITLES
THROUGH 2017

INTERCONTINENTAL CUP

1977
2000
2003
Total: 3

COPA SUDAMERICANA

2004
2005
Total: 2

COPA LIBERTADORES

Winner
1977
1978
2000
2001
2003
2007
Total: 6

Runner-up
1963
1979
2004
2012
Total: 4

SUPERCOPA SUDAMERICANA

1989
Total: 1

RECOPA SUDAMERICANA

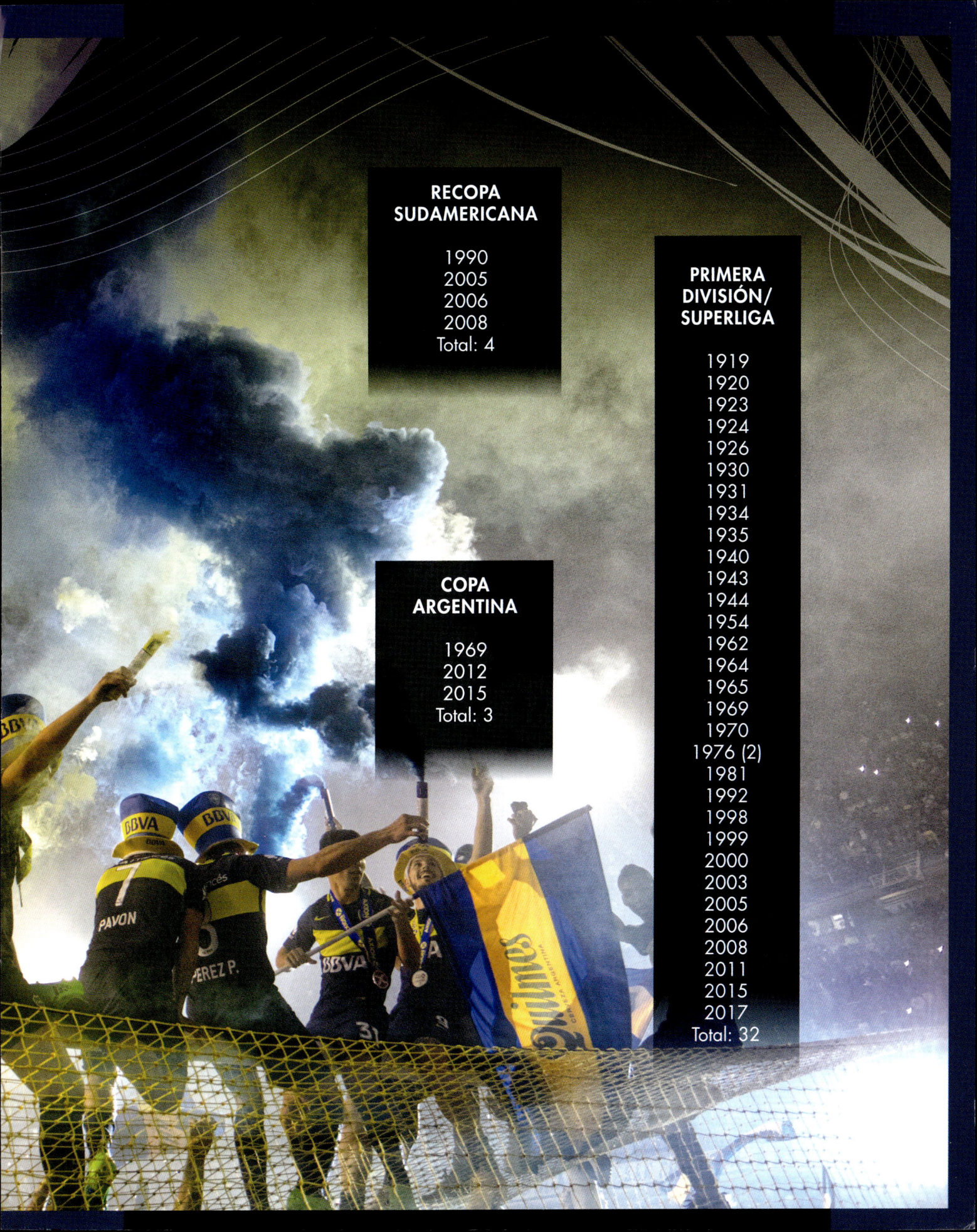

1990
2005
2006
2008
Total: 4

COPA ARGENTINA

1969
2012
2015
Total: 3

PRIMERA DIVISIÓN/ SUPERLIGA

1919
1920
1923
1924
1926
1930
1931
1934
1935
1940
1943
1944
1954
1962
1964
1965
1969
1970
1976 (2)
1981
1992
1998
1999
2000
2003
2005
2006
2008
2011
2015
2017
Total: 32

SELECTED BIBLIOGRAPHY

Dempsey, Luke. *Club Soccer 101: The Essential Guide to the Stars, Stats, and Stories of 101 of the Greatest Teams in the World.* New York: W. W. Norton, 2014.

Galeano, Eduardo. *Soccer in Sun and Shadow.* Translated by Mark Fried. New York: Nation Books, 2013.

Goldblatt, David, and Johnny Acton. *The Soccer Book: The Sport, the Teams, the Tactics, the Cups.* 3rd ed. New York: DK, 2014.

Mason, Tony. *Passion of the People?: Football in South America.* New York: Verso, 1995.

Richards, Joel. *Superclásico: Inside the Ultimate Derby.* Kindle edition. Seattle, Wash.: BackPage Press, 2013.

Wilson, Jonathan. *Angels with Dirty Faces: How Argentinian Soccer Defined a Nation and Changed the Game Forever.* New York: Nation Books, 2016.

WEBSITES

BOCA JUNIORS: FOOTBALL
http://www.bocajuniors.com.ar/futbol/noticias-futbol?lang=en
The Boca Juniors website includes game schedules and results, news, a detailed team history, and more.

OFFICIAL SITE OF THE ARGENTINE FOOTBALL ASSOCIATION
http://www.afa.org.ar/
The official AFA website previews upcoming games, notes the results and statistics of past matches, and highlights league news.

Note: Every effort has been made to ensure that the websites listed above are suitable for children, that they have educational value, and that they contain no inappropriate material. However, because of the nature of the Internet, it is impossible to guarantee that these sites will remain active indefinitely or that their contents will not be altered.

INDEX

Abbondanzieri, Roberto 39
Alarcón, Ricardo 22
Baglietto, Esteban 11
Barrios, Rubén Marcial 22
Bianchi, Carlos 31, 39
Brichetto, Juan 11
Caffarena, Victoriano "Toto" 18
Cherro, Roberto 36
Copa América 42
Copa Argentina 8, 43
Copa Libertadores 8, 25, 27-28, 34, 37, 39, 42, 43
Copa Sudamericana 8, 42
Farenga, Juan Antonio 11
   and Manuela 11
   and Teodoro 11
Felman, Darío 38
FIFA Club World Cup 8, 28, 33, 34, 38, 39, 42
   Intercontinental Cup 28, 33, 38, 39, 42
   Toyota Cup 33, 39
founding 11
Gatti, Hugo 28, 38
kits 11, 12
Kuko, Esteban 36
Maradona, Diego 28, 30–31, 39
Marzolini, Silvio 24, 41
Mastrángelo, Ernesto 38
Mayer, Marcos 14
McCarthy, Paddy 10–11
Mouzo, Roberto 27, 28
Musimessi, Julio Elías 23
Palermo, Martín 39, 42
Primera División (Superliga Argentina) 6, 13, 16, 18, 19, 20, 22, 23, 24, 27, 28, 30, 31, 33, 34, 37, 40, 41, 42, 43
Puerta 12 tragedy 25
Rattín, Antonio 41

Recopa Sudamericana 8
records 23, 33
Riquelme, Juan Román 31, 39, 42
Rogel, Roberto 37
Roma, Antonio 24, 27
Rosell, Julio Jorge 22
Salinas, Carlos Horacio 38
Sana, Santiago 11
Scarpatti, Alfredo 11
Schelotto, Guillermo Barros 39
Sosa, Carlos 40
South American Footballer of the Year 43
stadiums 12, 22, 24, 28, 34
   La Bombonera 22, 24, 28, 34
Suñé, Rubén 27
Superclásico 15–16, 19, 20, 24, 27, 31, 36, 37, 39, 40, 41, 43
Tarasconi, Domingo 36
team name 11, 12, 13
Tevez, Carlos 39, 43
Varallo, Francisco 37
Varela, Severino 40